The GREAT AMERICAN Mousical

JULIE ANDREWS EDWARDS & EMMA WALTON HAMILTON

Illustrated by Tony Walton

PUFFIN

The authors extend special thanks to Eliza Rand Damiecki and Naimy Hackett for their assistance with the Chinese and Italian phrases.

PUFFIN BOOKS

Published by the Penguin Group
Penguin Books Ltd, 80 Strand, London WC2R 0RL, England
Penguin Group (USA) Inc., 375 Hudson Street, New York, New York 10014, USA
Penguin Group (Canada), 90 Eglinton Avenue East, Suite 700, Toronto, Ontario, Canada M4P 2Y3
(a division of Pearson Penguin Canada Inc.)
Penguin Ireland, 25 St Stephen's Green, Dublin 2, Ireland (a division of Penguin Books Ltd)
Penguin Group (Australia), 250 Camberwell Road, Camberwell, Victoria 3124, Australia
(a division of Pearson Australia Group Pty Ltd)
Penguin Books India Pvt Ltd, 11 Community Centre, Panchsheel Park, New Delhi – 110 017, India
Penguin Group (NZ), 67 Apollo Drive, Mairangi Bay, Auckland 1310, New Zealand
(a division of Pearson New Zealand Ltd)
Penguin Books (South Africa) (Pty) Ltd, 24 Sturdee Avenue, Rosebank, Johannesburg 2196, South Africa

Penguin Books Ltd, Registered Offices: 80 Strand, London WC2R 0RL, England

penguin.com

First published in the USA by HarperCollins Children's Books 2006
First published in Great Britain in Puffin Books 2006
I

Text copyright © Julie Andrews Edwards and Emma Walton Hamilton, 2006
Illustrations copyright © Tony Walton, 2006

The moral right of the authors and illustrator has been asserted

Set in Centaur MT
Made and printed in England by Clays Ltd, St Ives plc

British Library Cataloguing in Publication Data
A CIP catalogue record for this book is available from the British Library

ISBN-13: 978–0–141–38277–7
ISBN-10: 0–141–38277–5

For our fellow theatre 'animals', with love.
—*J.A.E.*, *E.W.H.* and *T.W.*

Contents

Cast of Characters (*in order of appearance*)

 Harold – **the Character Actor**; plays the older roles

 Pippin – **the Student Apprentice**; the junior assistant

 Fritz – **the Assistant Stage Manager**; helps Enoch

 Enoch – **the Stage Manager**; in charge of the production backstage

 Bernardo – **the Hairstylist**; styles the wigs and hair

 Hysterium – **the Costume Shop Manager**; takes care of all the costumes

 Little June's Mom – a '**Stage Mother**'; ambitious for her daughter

Adelaide – **the Diva**; the star of
the show

 Emil – **the Director**; in charge of the
whole show

 Wendy – **the Ingénue**; the pretty
younger actress

 Curly – **the Comedian**; the funny guy
who dances

 Rose – **the Soubrette**; the good-hearted
supporting actress

 Sancho – **the Choreographer**; creates
the dances

 Sky – **the Lead**; the handsome male star

Pops – the Stage-door Mouse; guards
the actors' entrance to the theatre

 Charlemagne – the Set Designer; designs
the scenery

 Mrs Anna – the Costume Designer;
designs the clothes

 Lycus – the Lighting Designer; designs
the lighting that colours the show

 Raoul – the Sound Designer; in charge
of microphones and speakers

 Maestro Maraczek – the Musical Director;
conducts the orchestra

 Don Q – the Producer;
the boss, who pays for everything

Scud – the Rat; a thug

 Henry – a Country Professor; specializing in mouse lore

 Ping – the Apothecary's Nephew; works in a pharmacy in Chinatown

 Little June – a Child Actress

 Ping's Uncle – the Apothecary; owner of a pharmacy

 Fausto – the Owner of a Small Restaurant in Little Italy; loves opera

Additional Members of the Mouse Ensemble and Various Metropolitan Mice

Assorted Humans: Townspeople, Children and Others

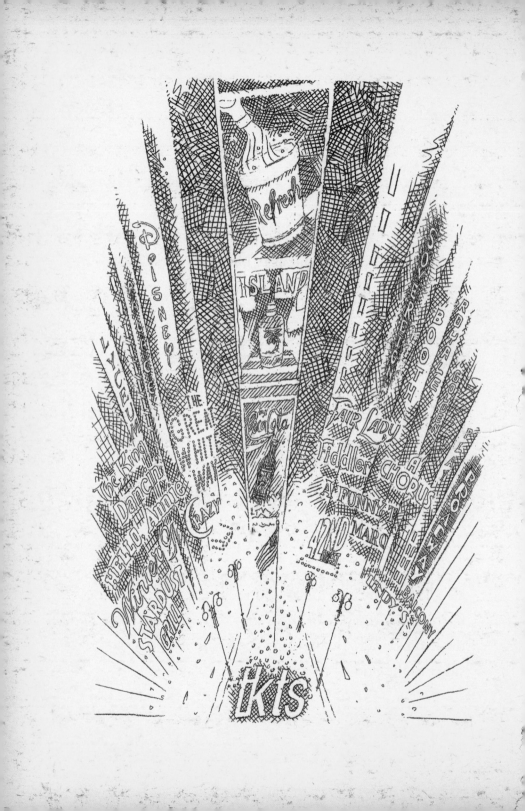

CHAPTER I

Warm-up

IF YOU COULD stand upon a faraway star and look down at planet Earth on a cloudless evening, you might just notice a glowing pool of light . . . and, chances are, that glow would be New York City. If you could leap from your star and fly down, down, down into the heart of that great metropolis, you would land in the most twinkling, sparkling place of all – Times Square. And, if you walked down any street in that area, you would be in the centre of the theatre district – Broadway, a place where magic happens every single night, and sometimes twice in a day.

The theatre where our story takes place was once very special and quite exquisite, which is why it was named the Sovereign. If you entered the lobby and passed through the swing doors into the chandeliered auditorium, you would feel a sense of wonder at all that had been contained therein: the thrilling music and dances, the words that expressed a thousand ideas, the costumes that rustled, the glowing lights that shone on the evocative scenery . . . You would understand that many lives had been touched here throughout the years.

If you walked down one of the carpeted aisles, out from under the gilt-edged balcony, past the tiers of red velvet seats and the boxed sections on either side of them, you would see the orchestra pit ahead of you,

the square of the proscenium and the gently curving apron of the stage. If by chance your eyes glanced to the right, and if you were *really* paying attention, you would spot a very small and carefully camouflaged door in the skirting board of the beaded wainscot.

On a night in late December, just after Christmas, when our tale begins, this little door was wide open. Leaning against the frame was a portly mouse dressed in corduroy knickerbockers, a faded waistcoat and striped bow tie. The little hair that remained on his head was long and wispy, but in spite of his shabby appearance there was a charisma about him — a certain grandeur, a slight pomposity, but the whole somehow compelling attention. His name was Harold. Behind him, peering around his considerable frame, was another mouse, Pippin — a youngster, clad in jeans, a faded T-shirt and a baseball cap turned backwards on his head. Around his neck was a thin piece of ribbon, to which was attached a small torch.

Harold was saying, 'The last night. I *hate* last nights . . . "parting is such sweet sorrow." But this show had a good long run.'

Pippin watched the dancing, tapping feet of the human performers, their shoes sparkling with sequins and bows, the chiffon skirts of the ladies swirling as their male partners twirled them around. The heads of the members of the orchestra were bobbing in rhythm, their shoulders leaning into the task of bringing the final song to a rousing finish. The music swelled, the voices onstage rose to a high note, and with a *whoosh!* the magnificent red velvet curtain swung down, the chains weighting its hem chinking and thudding on the stage, billowing and creating such a breeze that Pippin had to cling tightly to the back of Harold's trousers so as not to be blown away.

The applause from the audience was thunderous and, as he always did, Pippin thrilled to this moment — the music; the lights; the dry, warm smell of dust and make-up and paint — and he thought himself the luckiest mouse in the world to be a small part of it all.

'What happens now, Harold — now that this show has closed?' he asked. 'What's coming in next?'

Harold rubbed his chin. 'It's odd, but I haven't heard,' he replied. 'I've seen so many come and go, and

usually someone tells me what the next production will be –'

He was interrupted as an anxious, bespectacled young mouse dressed in black work clothes came skidding to a halt beside him.

'We've been looking for you everywhere!' he gasped breathlessly. 'Enoch says you have to come right away! Adelaide is at it again. Rehearsals are at a standstill, and you're the only one who can calm her down . . .'

The mice quickly closed the little door tightly behind them and scurried down a long, sloping corridor.

'Sorry, Fritz!' Pippin whispered as they followed Harold's ample frame.

'Really, Pippin! As an apprentice you should know you can't just run off to the human theatre anytime you feel like it. We open in just a few days! We need all paws on deck!'

They rounded a sharp corner and continued on down, into the bowels of the theatre, past the basement and the sub-basement, with its steaming pipes and electrical wires, and down again into the cavernous crawl spaces of the ancient building's very foundation. Nestled there, almost hidden between two towering pillars and long forgotten, was an exquisite miniature replica of the Sovereign Theatre as it once was.

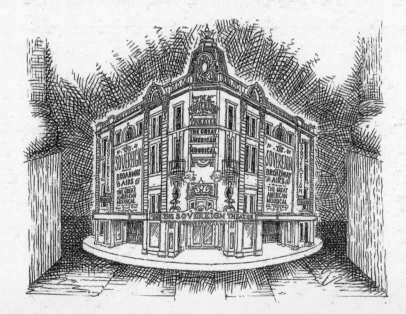

The actual building above had suffered many changes and many colours of paint. Windows had been blocked or boarded up, and its plaster was crumbling, but this little architect's model was pristine in appearance, albeit a trifle dusty, white and resplendent with gilt trim, curlicued mouldings, pillars, and balconies on its elegant facade. Beneath the classic line of the roof, carved cherubs smiled down to welcome all who entered. Large, colourful posters either side of the grand entrance read:

BROADWAY AIRS
A Tribute to the Great American Mousical
One Performance Only — New Year's Eve!

Harold, Pippin, and Fritz hurried through the stage door.

Enoch, the stage manager, was pacing impatiently by the entrance to the wardrobe department. 'Where have you two been!' he exclaimed. 'Of *all* the times to disappear . . .'

'Sorry, sorry,' Harold puffed. 'Couldn't resist a peek at the closing night upstairs. Furthering Pippin's education, you know. Now, what's up, dear boy?'

Enoch gestured helplessly towards the dressing-room area. A colossal argument could be heard emanating from behind the door marked with a gold star.

'Ah.' Harold nodded in understanding. 'Our leading lady is experiencing her usual pre-opening-night jitters.'

A slender mouse with dark, wavy hair came out from the wardrobe department, a wig in one hand, a brush in the other.

'Ooh la la!' he exclaimed. 'Sounds like our goddess is demanding a sacrifice.'

'Worse than that, Bernardo,' said Enoch with a sigh. 'It was suggested that young Wendy take over the flower-girl song. Now Adelaide's threatening not to go on at all.'

Harold snorted. 'Whose great mind made that poor choice?'

'Our director's, of course.' Enoch jumped as a loud crash came from behind the dressing-room door.

'Well, Emil should know better,' Harold declared. 'One does not replace a legendary star like Adelaide with an ingénue, no matter *how* talented she may be.'

'That's not all,' Fritz chimed in nervously. 'There's a problem with Adelaide's red dress in the staircase number. It's too tight.'

'No surprise.' Bernardo raised an eyebrow. 'She's been eating her way through rehearsals.'

'Well, this will require a little more than my usual bag of tricks,' Harold said. 'Happily, I am always prepared.' He produced a chocolate-covered peanut from his waistcoat pocket and blew a bit of lint off it. Placing his hand on the knob of the dressing-room door, he looked back at his colleagues and grinned. '"Once more unto the breach, dear friends!"' He took a deep breath and, arm extended, the chocolate peanut held high, charged into the dressing room and shut the door behind him.

CHAPTER 2

Rehearsal

'RIGHT! BACK TO work, everyone.' Enoch ushered Pippin, Fritz and Bernardo down the hall. 'We should let the company know what's happening. Get back to the prompt corner, will you, Fritzy?'

They entered the backstage area. Stagehands were pushing scenery into place. There was a babble of voices as twelve enthusiastic young mice dressed in Siamese costumes were being fussed over by concerned parents. Hysterium, the costume-shop manager, was dashing to and fro collecting headdresses

as the youngsters heedlessly tore them off. He spotted Enoch and ran to him.

'*Somebody* has to tell these kids to be more respectful of their costumes!' he fretted. 'I can't keep rushing upstairs to the human wardrobe department for snippets to make repairs. There just isn't time.'

Enoch opened his mouth to reply but was accosted by one of the mothers.

'Enoch!' she bellowed. 'This is a disaster! There's not been confusion like this since my little June was in *Felines!*'

A gasp went up from every mouse within earshot, followed by a great deal of spitting, the making of hex signs and turning around three times to rid the theatre of the forbidden word.

'Now, now, Mother,' Enoch said soothingly. 'If we all remain calm, we will get through this difficult time. Dress rehearsals are always the worst, as you well know.' He deftly plucked a young child from the path of some steps that were being wheeled forward.

The loudspeaker system clicked on, and Fritz's voice echoed hollowly in the cavernous backstage area. 'Stand by, please. We'll be beginning again momentarily.'

'As soon as Harold's finished "taming the shrew"!' Bernardo added, and ducked out of sight before Enoch could swat him.

'Is Adelaide going to come out, do you think?' Pippin asked anxiously.

'I'm sure she will,' Enoch said reassuringly.

Harold was saying, 'Darling, I know exactly how you feel.'

'Oh, *Harold!*' The theatre's leading lady and megastar rushed across her dressing room and flung her rather ample frame into his arms. 'You are the *only* one who *ever* understands!' Adelaide sobbed.

Harold glanced quizzically towards Emil, the dashingly dressed director of *Broadway Airs,* who was leaning wearily against Adelaide's dressing table and pouring himself a drink.

'I simply wondered if Adelaide might wish to appear generous and give young Wendy the chance she deserves,' he explained, his face betraying his frustration.

'I don't *feel* generous!' Adelaide said firmly, glaring at him. 'The flower girl is a character I'm perfectly able to manage, and I haven't shown the *youthful* side of my talent in years! I wonder what Don Q would say about this? Shall we send for him?'

'Now, now, Addie,' Harold said tenderly. 'No need to bother our producer. You'll always be eternally, sublimely youthful. You're a miracle, that's what you are.' He dabbed at her eyes with his handkerchief. 'These tears are not going to help that gorgeous voice, my pet. You must take care. How could we ever manage without you?'

'We couldn't, of course,' Emil said sincerely.

'Yes, well . . .' Adelaide sniffed, taking his handkerchief and delicately patting her neck with it. 'You have a funny way of showing your appreciation.'

'Look what I found for you!' With a flourish, Harold produced the chocolate-covered peanut.

Adelaide blinked with emotion. 'You are very dear, very sweet. I just wish I didn't feel so *fragile* these days . . .' She blew her nose vigorously.

'Nonsense! I've never seen you in more splendid form. You will be a tour de force on Monday night! Speaking of which,' Harold added tactfully, 'your boys are waiting onstage to rehearse the final number.

They're probably a bit fragile themselves by now, so . . .?'

'Oh, the poor darlings!' Adelaide was suddenly galvanized. Tossing the hair out of her eyes, she took the proffered peanut and popped it into her mouth. Opening the door, she swept down the hall towards the stage, hastily followed by a relieved Emil and a somewhat breathless Harold.

A pretty young mouse was coming towards them.

'Ah, Wendy!' Adelaide smiled sweetly at her. 'Don't you think you should wait till they fit, dear, before attempting to fill someone else's shoes?'

Emil winced and beat a hasty retreat to the front of the theatre. Wendy gasped and looked baffled. Then she glanced at Harold, her eyes spilling with tears.

'Oh, dear me. Oh, dearie, dearie me.' Harold patted his jacket distractedly as he fished about for his handkerchief, then realized that Adelaide had taken it onstage with her.

'Here, use mine,' a voice said. Curly, a young mouse in a brightly chequered suit, stepped forward and offered Wendy a piece of yellow silk from his breast pocket. 'Don't mind her, Wendy. I'm sure she doesn't mean it.'

'Curly's right, honey.' They were joined by Rose — a petite, curvaceous actress with an appealing, husky voice. 'Addie just needs to let off steam.'

A musical fanfare from a single trumpet sent them scurrying into the wings just in time to see Adelaide at the top of a long, curving flight of stairs. She smoothed the tight creases in her red dress. A feathered fan in one hand, the other lightly touching the railing, she paused for a moment, waiting for the great spotlight to find her. It flickered, then illuminated the steps just below her.

Emil's voice bellowed from the darkness of the auditorium. 'Find *Adelaide*, for goodness' sake!'

Sitting beside him at the technical table, Enoch whispered into his microphone, 'Wake up, up there!'

The spotlight wavered and finally settled on the star of the show. She began to walk down the staircase, and the orchestra struck up a rhythmic beat. At every level a young male dancer was waiting for her, one arm extended in greeting. Adelaide started to sing, ' "Hallo, fellas. Addie's back in town . . ." ' Her voice sounded a little ragged, but there was no doubting her star quality.

Reaching the stage, she moved to the right. The spotlight moved to the left. Adelaide threw up her hands in exasperation and froze in her tracks. The dancers barrelled into her.

'Stop, *stop*, STOP!' Emil's voice called again. 'Sancho! *What* is happening?'

The slim choreographer bounded up the steps at the side of the orchestra pit. 'Darlings!' he cried, running his hands through his long hair. 'Let's get this straight. Boys move to the left. *Adelaide* goes to the right.'

One of the dancers mumbled, 'If we spent a little more time *rehearsing* . . .'

Sancho nudged him hard to shut him up, lined up the other dancers, and turned to the orchestra conductor. 'From the bridge of the song, Maestro, if you please.'

The orchestra tentatively began again and, fumbling with her words for a moment, Adelaide found the melody and continued on.

Sancho beat time with his foot and clapped his hands. 'A little faster, please. A one, two, *three*! Boys crossing *now*. NO! *Behind* Adelaide . . .'

One of the dancers hesitated. Adelaide tried to outguess him, and they glanced off each other. Adelaide stumbled backwards. Reaching for the banister rail of the stairs, she tripped on the long train of her red dress. There was a terrible ripping sound as a seam split open across her backside. The dancers gasped. The great spotlight wavered and then moved tactfully away.

'Hold it, HOLD IT!' Sancho and Emil yelled at exactly the same moment. The orchestra, sounding confused, gradually stopped playing.

Adelaide screamed, 'That's it! I've had it! Rehearse if you want. I'll see you tomorrow.' She brushed past Pippin and the spectators in the wings and stormed off to her dressing room, clutching at the large tear in her dress as she went.

There was a moment's silence. Then Bernardo said wickedly, 'Ho hum! What a pickle! I thought the grand *opening* was supposed to be on Monday night!'

CHAPTER 3

Overture

EMIL YELLED, 'We'll rehearse this again later! We've *got* to move on. NEXT!'

Sitting beside him at the technical rehearsal table in the audience, Enoch pressed buttons on his electrical panel and spoke into his headset. 'Fritz, tell Curly to stand by.' He pressed another button. 'Clear the stage, please. Bring in the number three drop . . . thank you. And cue orchestra . . . GO.'

Curly made his entrance and began to sing and dance a gentle soft-shoe with grace and style. Members of the company who were assembled in the theatre seats awaiting their rehearsal gave him an enthusiastic ovation.

Emil asked Enoch to call Wendy to the stage. She walked out, shielding her eyes from the bright lights as she scanned the auditorium, looking for the director.

'Wendy, darling,' he called to her. 'We need to try Adelaide's flower-girl song so that we can at least practise the lighting cues. Would you walk it through for us? The orchestra would appreciate the rehearsal as well.'

'Oh, of course,' Wendy said obligingly.

Standing backstage, Pippin, Curly, Rose and Fritz watched Wendy's enchanting rendition of the song. They were joined by a tall, handsome mouse in a pinstripe suit.

'She's good,' he observed, lifting an eyebrow appraisingly.

Rose nodded. 'She's better than good, Sky. It should be *her* number, not Adelaide's.'

There were cheers and whistles from the cast and crew as Wendy finished.

Enoch removed his headset and turned to the director. 'Would it be all right, Emil, if we called it a night? Adelaide has left the theatre, so there's no way to finish rehearsing the staircase number now — it's too complicated. I'm recommending we start with that first thing tomorrow.'

'Good idea,' Emil concurred. He called, 'That's all for tonight, company! Get some rest.'

Curly approached Wendy. 'You were terrific, Wendy. I — I was wondering if you'd like to —'

Sky brushed past him.

'Hey, babe,' he intoned in his mellifluous baritone. 'You were absolutely *delicious* . . . right on the mark! I

have a couple of thoughts about it that I'd like to share with you. How 'bout I escort you home?'

Curly looked crestfallen. 'But . . . I was just . . .'

Sky draped his jacket around Wendy's shoulders. 'Here you go, babe. It's cold out there. You shouldn't be walking home alone anyway.'

'Oh . . .' Wendy hesitated.

'I *insist*.' Sky took her arm. 'We go the same way anyway. 'Night, all!' He waved casually as he ushered Wendy down the hall.

Curly was left standing with his mouth open, his arm extended as if to stop them.

Rose placed a paw on Curly's shoulder. 'Ain't he a piece of work?' she declared huskily. 'Too bad he's such a hunk. But don't worry, kid. As soon as the novelty wears off, you'll get your girl back . . . and I'll get my guy.'

Curly blushed. 'Oh, Rose – I can't compete with our leading man.'

'Sure you can.' She winked. 'If I wasn't already in love with him, I'd fall for you myself. See, I know how heartache feels.'

CHAPTER 4

Lights Dim

THE THEATRE EMPTIED rapidly. Enoch, Fritz and Pippin were left to ensure that all was tidied and left in readiness for the following day's rehearsal.

Pippin said, 'Fritz and I can finish up here, Enoch. Why don't you take off and get some rest?'

Enoch nodded, grateful. 'Good lad. If you'd just sweep up, bring out the ghost light, and check around. Then come on home. We'll leave some crumbs out for you.' He shrugged into his threadbare jacket and lifted his ancient briefcase, crammed with papers.

'Fritzy – make sure the auditorium is clean, will you?'

'No problem.' The assistant stage manager picked up a waste-paper basket and headed out to the front of the house. Pippin fetched a long metal stand with a caged light bulb on top of it and rolled it on to the darkened stage. He plugged in the attached cable and the light flickered on, casting a cold, white glow over everything and lengthening the shadows. After the chaos of rehearsals, the Sovereign seemed eerily quiet.

The young mouse stood centre stage in a shaft of light, drinking in the atmosphere, savouring the moment of having it all to himself. He gazed out into the empty theatre and felt the magic envelop him.

On a whim, he struck a dramatic pose: knees bent, body turned sideways, head down, one hand at his hip, the other on his cap. 'Ta-da!' he said softly.

'*Nice!*' Fritz's voice came from somewhere out in the darkness.

Pippin grinned, embarrassed. 'Some day,' he called back jauntily. 'Maybe.'

'I'm outta here,' Fritz stated. 'See you tomorrow.'

Pippin swept the stage and walked through the

building, tidying the Green Room where the actors socialized backstage, closing dressing-room doors, and turning out lights as he went.

He retrieved his baseball jacket and the scarf that his mother had knitted for him from the wardrobe department. Then he stopped to talk with Pops, the elderly stage-door mouse who, traditionally, was always the last person to leave.

'There's an icy draught upstairs,' Pops said. 'Must be close to freezing outside.'

'Someone said it will snow soon.'

'Yup! Oh – be careful going through the human theatre,' Pops cautioned. 'They set a new kind of trap in the costume shop. One of them supposedly humane kinds. With peanut butter and cheese inside. It nearly fooled *me*.'

'Wow!' Pippin suddenly realized how hungry he was.

'Yup!' Pops said again. 'Also, I think some people are still around up there. I heard footsteps.'

'I'll be careful,' Pippin reassured him. ''Night, Pops. Thanks!'

Pippin climbed up the three flights of damp, cold stairs to the big theatre. He tiptoed by the human costume department, rank with sweat and hairspray and cleaning fluid. He smelt the cheese in the mousetrap before he even saw it and, in spite of the grumbling of his empty stomach, he didn't go near the evil contraption. He was just scuttling towards the big stage door when a loud thump made him freeze in his tracks.

A baseball with signatures on it bounced down the hallway and rolled past, missing him by a millimetre.

A human hand reached to retrieve it, followed by the freckled face of a young boy, who stared at Pippin in surprise. Mesmerized, the boy and the mouse gazed at each other for a long moment, their

noses almost touching. The ball rolled on and lodged beneath a radiator.

'Dad!' The boy's face disappeared. 'I saw a mouse!'

'Not surprising,' a deep voice replied. 'The place is riddled with them. But they'll be scurrying soon. They'll never know what hit 'em.'

Pippin shuddered and made a dash for the exit hole by the big door to the street. He came out into the night air and leaned against a cornerstone of the building, his heart pounding. Usually the mice kept as far away from humans as possible, and this encounter with the boy had been too close.

What was it that the father had been saying? 'They'll be scurrying soon.' What could he have meant? Something about the phrase gave Pippin a chill.

The little mouse took a deep breath of fresh air and looked up at the sky far, far above him. He thought of his family back home in the countryside and wondered if they were looking at the same stars. They had been so generous supporting his dream of working in the theatre, helping him to stow away on the bus to New York. Even though they were as poor as churchmice usually are, they had pressed into his paws a few hard-earned scraps of cheese for the journey. If only they could see what he was seeing now.

The lights in Times Square were flashing on and off, some chasing over the buildings in marvellous patterns, others miraculously exploding into cascading showers. On top of one of the tallest buildings, balanced on the tip of a pole, was a big, shining, silver ball. Pippin knew that on Monday evening – the same night as their performance of *Broadway Airs* – the ball would come sliding down on the final stroke of midnight to usher in a brand-new year.

Most amazing of all was an enormous pair of illuminated Mickey Mouse ears, which towered over

everything, changing colours rapidly – red, green, red, green, black. Pippin marvelled at the thoughtfulness of mankind in erecting such a monument to the most famous mouse performer of all time, and he resolved anew to justify his family's faith in him. One day he would make his own contribution to mouse theatre history.

He set off down the street, heading towards the humble dwelling where he was staying with Enoch and his family. He was careful to keep in the shadow of the buildings, but happily there were few people around. He wondered what Harold, Curly, Wendy, Adelaide and Rose were doing at this moment.

Harold was in fact snoring mightily in his overstuffed armchair. Curly was practising a dance in his garret high above the city. He wore a top hat and carried a cane and, watching his reflection in a long mirror, he thought of Wendy and sighed. Cradling the cane as if it were she, he danced and danced.

Wendy was sitting at her window, gazing into the night and thinking about the events of the day. Sky had been so kind, so attentive to her. Why had Adelaide been so unfriendly?

Adelaide was seated at her dressing table, removing her make-up and picking sadly at cheese and chocolates from a tray nearby.

Rose was alone in bed, wishing that Sky would change his ways. She turned over restlessly and looked at the clock on her bedside table.

Pippin let himself into Enoch's tiny abode and tiptoed carefully past the open door of the bedroom, where the kindly stage manager, his wife and six children were cuddled together, sleeping blissfully in one large bed. He nibbled at the crumbs that had been left out for him, then climbed into the padded sardine tin that was his bed.

Long before the pale pink light of dawn rose over the city, he too was fast asleep, twitching occasionally as he dreamed innocently of happy days to come.

CHAPTER 5

Act One

THE FOLLOWING afternoon all was hustle and bustle again at the mouse theatre. Seamstresses were working on Adelaide's torn costume, Hysterium was mending the Siamese headdresses, Bernardo was dressing his wigs. The performers were waiting onstage for Adelaide to arrive. Emil was in the auditorium giving notes to his creative team: Charlemagne, the set designer; Mrs Anna, who was responsible for costumes; Lycus, the lighting designer; Raoul, the sound man; Maestro Maraczek, the orchestra conductor; Sancho, the choreographer;

and Enoch, who was taking everything down, scribbling furiously on his notepad.

There was a loud commotion in the wings as Adelaide burst on to the stage, arms laden with a script and several shopping bags full of snacks, which she dumped unceremoniously by the footlights.

'I know, I know. I'm late!' she announced dramatically. 'Don't nag! I overslept . . . didn't even stop for breakfast. I'm a *wreck*, but here I am.'

'Good, good,' Emil called. 'Let's get started!'

As everyone moved to their places, Pippin tugged at Enoch's sleeve.

'Junie's mom wants to speak with you backstage,' he whispered. 'Fritz said please come quickly.' Enoch rolled his eyes and headed for the prompt corner.

'She just brushed past me, trod on my toe, and then complained that *I* was in *her* way!' the mother was saying to Fritz as they arrived. 'I really think you should say something to her. Who does she think she is!'

'She's our leading lady, dear,' Enoch said with infinite patience. 'She carries the entire show on her shoulders and is under tremendous pressure right now. We all know she can be maddening, selfish, demanding – but there is absolutely no one else who can light up a stage the way she does. We'd be lost without her.' He took up Fritz's headset and, putting it on, he called, 'Stand by for Adelaide's number and the finale, please. Whenever you're ready, Maestro.'

Maestro Maraczek tapped his baton against his music stand to prepare members of the orchestra, and the rehearsal began. This time Adelaide's staircase routine proceeded smoothly, and afterwards row upon row of actors lined up to sing the last rousing song, 'Sunset Over Broadway', and to rehearse their bows.

Suddenly – inexplicably – the stage began to shake.

A low, menacing rumble came from above, and the hanging lamps in the rafters rattled and swung together, their coloured lenses breaking into shards. Members of the company screamed and ducked as plaster and glass rained down on the stage like a shower. Parents and stagehands ran on to the set and carried children out of harm's way.

Just as suddenly the shaking stopped.

Enoch rushed out. 'Is everyone all right? Anyone hurt?'

No one was.

Adelaide said heatedly, 'Can anyone explain what that *was*?'

No one could.

Emil called, 'I suggest that we go and find out –' but he never finished the sentence, for the shaking began again, worse this time.

One end of a hanging painted drop broke free and fell at an angle, skewering into the stage, narrowly missing Adelaide. She looked up, indignant. 'HEY!' she called out to no one in particular. Splinters of wood, dust and debris hurtled into the wings, where Wendy was standing. Curly launched himself in front

⌣:37:⌣

of her, pushing her out of danger in the nick of time. She gasped and looked at him, wide-eyed.

'Curly, thank you *so* much! What on earth is happening?'

By now most of the mice were dashing for the

stairs leading to the human theatre. They streamed down the main corridor, where the rumbling noise was even louder, and spilled on to the pavement outside the big stage door, tumbling and falling over one another as they skidded to a halt.

Manoeuvring back and forth in an attempt to park
next to the kerb was a monster of a machine, electric
yellow, with giant caterpillar tracks instead of wheels.
A cab and a vast crane formed the superstructure.
Hanging from the crane was a thick chain, with a

huge, black concrete ball at the end of it.

'What is it, what is it?' the mice children asked,
gazing up in awe.

Everyone had a question. 'What does it do?' 'What
is it there for?' 'What can it mean?'

Pops held up a paw for silence. 'Listen up, folks. Perhaps I can explain.' He told them that, as he was leaving the previous evening, he had heard human voices in the main corridor upstairs: a father and his son. Their conversation didn't make much sense to him.

'The father was saying odd things such as "We own the theatre now", and they talked about a "television studio" and "big bucks",' Pops continued. 'They used words like "demolition" and "new construction" . . .'

Pippin gasped as he remembered the phrase *he* had heard last night: 'They'll be scurrying soon.' He raised an arm for attention and told the mice of his own experience with the people. 'It must mean that the Sovereign is going to be torn down to make way for a new building!' he said with horror. 'I guess that's what this huge machine is for . . .'

They all began to speak at once. What would happen to their beautiful little theatre? Would there be enough time to produce the big benefit? Would they all be out of work? What could they possibly do?

Emil raised his voice over the babble. 'Hey, folks!

This is all speculation and hearsay. I think we're overreacting. Until we know for sure, I suggest we press ahead with our rehearsals. We're way behind as it is . . . Shall we?' He indicated the stage door. 'We'll attract attention out here.'

The mice heeded his advice and went back inside. All, that is, except Adelaide. She had been truly shaken by the incident of the falling scenery and how narrowly it had missed her, and now the wrecking-ball issue seemed like the last straw.

Dazed with fright and trembling from lack of food, she felt strangely disoriented.

'Darling,' Harold called to her. 'Are you coming?'

She snapped into focus. 'Yes. Yes. A last breath of fresh air. I'm on my way.'

Tottering unsteadily into the theatre and along the corridor towards the basement stairs, she wondered what she could do to get rid of the dizzy feeling in her head. She should have eaten breakfast. As she passed the human wardrobe department, the smell of cheese and peanut butter suddenly tickled her nostrils. Without a moment's hesitation, she made an abrupt left turn.

The Havahart mousetrap stood in the middle of the room. Drawn by a terrible compulsion, Adelaide stood in front of it, intoxicated by the perfume of the goodies inside, her nose quivering, her mouth watering. One nibble of that delicious-looking cheese would set her right again, she was sure of it. The peanut butter would soothe her tummy – and her nerves. If she was very, very careful and could just inch her way into the box and take the *gentlest* bite . . .

Her pearly-white teeth closed on the cheese and

suddenly — *wham!* — the door slammed shut and she was caught. With a scream, Adelaide spun around, her heart feeling as though it would explode in her chest.

In panic, she felt her way around the interior walls of the trap. There must be a way to get out. *Someone must know how to open the door.*

'HELP!' Adelaide gave the call her best shot. 'Harold? Somebody . . . HALLO-O! I'm in here.' She listened for the patter of little paws but all was silent, and though Adelaide continued to cry for help until she was hoarse, there was not a mouse within earshot to come to her aid.

CHAPTER 6

Interval

IN THE MOUSE THEATRE below, the broken scenery had been cleared away and Emil and the assembled cast were onstage, waiting for Adelaide to return.

'She merely said she needed some fresh air,' Harold stated as Emil gave him a quizzical look. The dancers sat down to relax and stretch, and the children were sent to their dressing rooms for a snack.

'Could she have gone back home?' Fritz asked Enoch.

Enoch frowned. 'She's been so stressed lately . . .'

'I have to confess I'm worried about her,' Harold

said quietly to Sky. 'She's always been a handful, but she's looking a bit sad these days, don't you think?'

'Yeah. I remember when we were younger; she seemed easier to put up with. She was such a knockout.' Sky smiled at Wendy as she passed.

Little June's mother had been eavesdropping. 'Well, she's certainly a diva now. She's probably having a hissy fit in Don Q's office,' she said caustically.

'Nah, that would mess up her hair.' Bernardo winked at them as he swept by.

'All right, that's *enough*, everyone,' Enoch said. 'Pippin, go topside again, will you, and check?'

'I'll come with you,' Harold offered. 'She may need me.'

Upstairs, imprisoned in the mousetrap, Adelaide had consumed most of the cheese and peanut butter and was now feeling rather queasy. She sat glumly in a corner, wondering if anyone below would think to look for her in the human costume shop. Suddenly she heard a young person's voice.

'I'll be right there, Dad! I'm looking for my Yankees ball! I know it's here somewhere!'

Adelaide started up, quiveringly alert, as footsteps came horrifyingly close. There was a moment's silence, and she wondered if perhaps they had gone away. Then directly above her the voice said, 'Huh?'

All at once she felt the box being lifted into the air, and she scrambled for traction as it was shaken vigorously from side to side. Teeth rattling, she let out a shriek just as Harold and Pippin skidded to a halt by the doorway.

'Whoops! Careful!' Harold flung out an arm to prevent Pippin from going any further. Both mice ducked out of sight beneath the radiator.

'Poor little mousie!' said the human voice, and Pippin recognized the boy he had seen the previous night. He was holding the box to his eye, peering at Adelaide through the mesh siding.

'Harold! She's in there – she's in the *box!*' Pippin whispered urgently. 'She must have gone for the peanut butter and cheese!'

Harold was appalled. '"Frailty, thy name is woman!"' he groaned.

'Don't worry, mousie,' the boy continued. 'I won't let you get smashed by the wrecking ball.' He turned

and headed for the big stage door, the mousetrap held gently between his hands.

'Yegads! We've got to stop him!' Harold gasped, and he and Pippin bravely scurried after the boy. As they came out on to the street, a large pair of men's work boots missed them by a whisker.

'Watch it, son!' boomed a voice above them. 'This is a construction site now. You don't want to get too close.'

Bright-orange plastic fencing rattled past their noses. The mice pressed themselves against the side of the building and watched as the work boots nudged it into position, forming a barricade around the giant wrecking crane.

The boy was saying, 'When does the demolition start?'

'Not for a few days. Big storm coming – gotta wait for it to pass. No one can work in a blizzard.'

'It makes me kinda sad to see this come down.' The boy gazed at the theatre's crumbling facade. 'It must have been a pretty cool place once.'

Pippin and Harold exchanged glances. So Pops had heard right – the theatre *was* going to be demolished.

The man in the work boots nodded, hooking the fencing on to steel posts. 'The wife and I came here on our honeymoon. Saw *The Rain King*. It was great, I tell you.'

Harold whispered sadly, 'That was one of the Sovereign's longest-running hits . . .'

The man continued, 'The place has been plastered over so many times, you can't tell what it originally looked like. Now we'll never know.'

'My dad's gonna make it into a TV studio.'

'Huh.' The workman snorted. 'Progress!'

'I know. I wish it didn't have to happen.'

'Son! Let's go!' A pair of black designer boots crunched into view. 'The weather's closing in fast. Did you find your baseball?'

'No, Dad!'

'Well, we have to hit the road while we still can. We'll come back for a last look after the snow clears. Hurry now.' The dapper boots walked away.

The young boy quickly thrust Adelaide's box towards the construction worker. 'Could you do me a favour? There's a little mouse in here that I rescued. Would you set it free somewhere on your way home? Please? Dad wouldn't understand . . .'

The workman glanced at the box, then chuckled. 'Sure, kid. Toss it on the seat of my truck there. I'll take care of it.'

The boy ran to the kerb and passed the mousetrap through the open window of the truck's cab.

Moments later the man in the work boots clambered aboard and the vehicle roared into life. Harold and Pippin watched in horror as the truck rolled slowly away, carrying with it the star of their show. Powerless to intervene, they watched it recede until it disappeared into the gently falling snow.

CHAPTER 7

Entr'acte

THE STREET SEEMED chillingly quiet, eerily
still.

Harold placed a paw on Pippin's shoulder.
'Son . . . *this* is the end of the world as we have known
it. One of the shining lights of the theatre has just
gone out of our lives.' The elderly mouse seemed
suddenly frail. 'And, oh my stars! How do we tell
everyone that their show is finished? Over! Without
Adelaide . . .' Head bowed, he turned and walked
slowly back into the theatre.

Pippin followed, dreadfully concerned. He patted

Harold gently on the back in a futile attempt to console him.

Once below stairs the actor sank into a large gilt throne that had been placed in the centre of the mouse stage.

'"Angels and ministers of grace defend us!"' he cried piteously as performers, technicians, children and musicians anxiously clustered around him. 'She's gone!' He raised his arm as if to push away the dreadful memory. 'She – she disappeared into a veil . . . a misty wreath of white and grey, enfolding her . . . "a foul and pestilent congregation of vapours"!' He buried his face in his paws.

'Steady, Harold!' Emil produced a silver flask from

his hip pocket. He poured a thimbleful of elderberry wine and handed it to the distraught actor. 'Take it easy, now. Just cut to the chase and tell us what happened.'

'I cannot. I simply can't. Pippin – *you* elaborate.' Emotionally spent, Harold leaned back in the chair and took a large swig of the smooth, tummy-warming nectar.

Pippin began, 'Well . . . we found Adelaide in the trap upstairs, you see. In the human costume shop. She was locked inside and couldn't get out –'

'Though I pounded and heaved at the door!' Harold momentarily regained his strength. 'Suddenly – footsteps were coming toward us. Thump, *thump*. Thud, THUD! There was nowhere to hide. The trap was picked up. I tore after them – two humans. *Huge.* Strong. There was a third man outside. A giant, with enormous boots! What could I do?' He drained the thimble of its contents.

Pippin blinked, and then continued. 'I think the man outside works that big crane we saw. The boy spoke to him and asked him to take the trap away –'

'Far, FAR away,' Harold interrupted again. 'The

boy *hurled* it into a vast truck, Adelaide was crying out – screaming! "Distill'd almost to jelly with the act of fear." Poor darling . . .' The actor bit his lip and, one paw on his heart, held out the thimble. Emil refilled it.

'Then what?' the director asked gently.

'Then –' Pippin began again.

'*Then*, of course, I tried to save her!' Harold was now on a roll. 'I practically *threw* myself in front of the truck. But, alas . . . 'twas all to no avail. She's gone, I tell you. Kidnapped. Taken from us.'

There was a gasp from the assembled cast and crew, then an awed silence. Everyone looked at Emil.

He bowed his head a moment, then looked at them, his eyes dark and troubled.

'It is time to send for Don Q,' he said quietly. 'Our producer has to be informed of this terrible tragedy. He will help us decide what is to be done.'

Half an hour later, an elderly mouse with an imposing demeanour stood before the company. He was immaculately dressed. A flowing cape swung from his shoulders, partially covering his dark suit and the shining fob watch that dangled from his waistcoat. He carried a silver-handled cane, and upon his steel-grey hair he wore a top hat.

'So, dear friends. This is indeed our darkest hour,' Don Q said gravely, his voice deep and resonant. 'We have a wrecking ball hanging above our heads. Our leading lady has been taken from us. Our benefit looks to be ruined. Even if our beloved theatre remains intact a few days more, can we possibly proceed without Adelaide? I welcome your thoughts.'

Emil was the first to speak. 'Art *must* endure, of

course. Even if we stand in the rubble, we should still perform.'

Enoch said, 'It is the one thing that binds us together – the one thing that tells us who we are.'

Curly said, 'I agree. Other mice would wish us to set an example.'

Rose spoke next. 'If we work together, our spirit can *never* be crushed.'

Maestro Maraczek added, 'Music soothes and restores the soul.'

'But without Adelaide . . .?' Sky shook his head.

There was a pause.

Pippin said tentatively, 'I thought the tradition was "The show must go on"?'

Wendy nodded. 'If we don't go on, then evil triumphs!'

'But how?' 'But *how!*' Everyone wanted to know. 'What can we possibly *do?*'

'We will find a way,' Emil reassured them. 'We will stand in the light and be a beacon of hope.'

Harold held up his paw. 'Besides,' he said soberly, '*Adelaide* would want it.'

There was a chorus of assent.

Don Q said warmly, 'Bravo! Indeed she would. So, how shall we proceed?'

Emil rubbed his brow. 'Here's what we could do. Wendy, you could take on Adelaide's love duet with Sky, and of course you'd have to do the flower-girl song.' Wendy nodded. 'Rose . . . do you think you could handle the comedy routine with Curly?'

'You bet, honey.' Rose grinned and winked at Curly.

Little June's mother asked, 'Who'd do the schoolroom number with the children?'

'I could do that, too,' Rose offered. 'I sang it in music class once.'

Emil nodded his approval. 'We'd have to tweak other things as well – but I think it's all possible.'

'But what about the finale?' Enoch enquired. 'The staircase number.'

Emil sighed. 'No disrespect to anyone here, but that was *pure* Adelaide. It was her song, her role, her finest moment. I need time to come up with something.'

Don Q said, 'Well. We certainly have enough to keep us busy, but time is a luxury we don't have. You'll have to think fast. Shall we now take a vote? All in favour of continuing say aye.'

'Aye!' 'AYE!' The cry came from all sides. 'The show *must* go on!'

'Any opposed?'

Silence.

Don Q nodded and smiled. 'Thank you, my friends. So be it. In spite of all, we shall proceed. In Adelaide's honour.'

There was a roaring, unanimous cheer.

'FOR ADELAIDE!'

CHAPTER 8

Act Two

ADELAIDE HAD BEEN bumped and jostled in the mousetrap for what seemed like hours. Still in her rehearsal robe, she was chilled to the marrow and more frightened than she had ever been in her life. What must they be thinking at the theatre? Would they ever know what had happened to her?

She could tell she was in some kind of vehicle. It was rolling and rattling its way over something gridlike when suddenly it swerved to the right and came to a halt. She felt the box being picked up, and a voice mumbled, 'This is as far as you go, mouse.

You're outta the city, and now you're outta here.'

The box hurtled through space. It landed in the snow with a terrible crunch, and the trapdoor burst open. Adelaide was so jarred that she saw stars.

When she regained her senses, she emerged trembling and tentative into a world unlike any she had ever seen. A lamp somewhere above her swung to and fro in the wind, casting an eerie yellow beam across tall wooden posts and packing crates. There were the sounds of water lapping and timbers creaking, and a bell clanged somewhere in the distance.

It was snowing hard, and the little mouse wondered what she could do, where she could go to protect herself. She wouldn't last long in this weather.

She nearly jumped out of her skin as a voice behind her said, 'What's a nice gal like you doing in a place like this?'

Wheeling around, she found herself face-to-face with an enormous, oily-looking rat. An ugly scar disfigured his face, and one eyelid was almost closed. He squinted at her, his head tilted to one side, then advanced closer.

Adelaide backed up against a crate, her heart thumping wildly.

'Whaddya got for me, little lady?' He leered, an approving glint in his one good eye.

Casting about her wildly, she spotted the broken trap lying on the ground. 'There!' she said, pointing a trembling finger. 'In the box. There's some delicious cheese. Take it!'

Watching her suspiciously, the rat took a few steps towards the box. Adelaide seized her chance and made a break for it. Running blindly, she rounded a corner and slammed full tilt into someone who caught her by the shoulders and said, 'Whoa! Careful now!

What's your hurry?'

It was another mouse.

'Oh, please . . . let me go, I beg you!' Adelaide

was almost out of her mind with panic.

The stranger looked surprised. 'I think *you* ran into *me* —' he began, then caught sight of the thug rat who had appeared around the corner and was approaching fast.

Adelaide babbled, 'There! He — he . . . Oh, for pity's sake, help me!'

Quickly grasping the situation, the newcomer stepped protectively in front of her. 'You're a little far afield tonight, aren't you, Scud? Might I suggest you leave the neighbourhood before it's too late? I'm sure the Sons of Vermin would be only too happy to tell the Big Cheese you were on his dock . . .'

The ugly rodent hesitated.

'Be off with you, before I sound the alert!' the stranger commanded.

The rat hissed his frustration, then backed away and melted into the darkness.

Adelaide gasped her thanks, sobbing with relief.

'It was nothing, my dear. But you shouldn't be walking these docks after dark, let alone in this weather. Shall I escort you home?'

'That's just it!' Adelaide blubbed. 'I've been

kidnapped – taken on an endless journey in a prison chamber. I've no idea where I am! My home is on Broadway . . .'

'My word!' Her rescuer seemed impressed. 'You *have* come a long way.'

'Worse than that, our show opens tomorrow night! They'll be lost without me . . . Oh, what am I to do!' she wailed.

'I – I'm not sure I completely understand . . .'

'What part don't you understand?' Adelaide replied crisply. 'I'm in a very important stage production. I'm the *star!* And instead of being with my company and preparing for tomorrow's performance, I find myself here in this lawless, miserable, filthy . . .' She was unable to continue and brushed furiously at her eyes with her sleeve.

'Well, one thing's for sure. We're not going to solve anything by standing out here in the snow.' The kindly mouse took her arm and gently escorted her away from the docks. 'You've been through a terrible ordeal. I can provide a warm drink and a roof over your head while you pull your thoughts together. It's a humble place, I'm afraid . . . but it's safe.'

Adelaide looked at him. Her companion had a pleasant face, framed by a pair of wire-rimmed spectacles. He was tall and extremely thin, and instead of a coat he was wrapped in several well-worn sweaters, with a couple of long scarves wound about his neck. 'What were *you* doing on the dock?' she asked, curious.

'Taking a short cut home, trying to beat the storm,' he replied simply. 'I was teaching an evening class. I normally give the waterfront a wide berth, but I think it's fortunate that the elements encouraged me to venture there this evening. Ah, here we are . . .'

They had reached a dilapidated old building and, passing beneath an iron grating set in the mildewed stones of the wall, Adelaide found herself in a mouse-size suite of rooms. A single lamp in the ceiling illuminated stack upon stack of shelves, filled to overflowing with books. There was a desk with papers scattered across it, and an old and well-worn couch.

'My name is Henry,' said her escort as he touched a match to the coals in a little fireplace. 'May I know yours?'

'Adelaide,' she replied, drawn to the flames as they began to sputter and burn.

'We'll soon have some hot tea.' Henry filled a kettle and set it on top of the coals. He swept some books from the couch and indicated that she should be seated. 'You say you are in the theatre . . . how truly exhilarating. I confess I have never been to a Broadway show – that's too far for me, though of course I have read just about every play. I'm a great enthusiast.'

Adelaide shivered. 'Do you have anything to eat?' she asked.

'Oh, dear me.' He took an old cookie tin from a shelf and peered into it. 'I'm not much of a gourmet, I'm afraid. The best I can offer is a couple of oyster crackers.'

'They'll do.' Adelaide practically inhaled them. Henry handed her a mug of thickly sweetened tea, and the liquid coursed through her body. She leaned back against the cushions of the couch and began to relax for the first time that day.

Looking at the books on every wall, she mused, 'Henry . . . would that be as in "Higgins"?'

Henry smiled. 'Actually, it's as in "Thoreau".' My grandparents inhabited an old cabin near Walden Pond.' He stirred the coals and removed a scarf. 'I'm a professor of mouse lore. But please tell me more about yourself. Would I have read your play, perchance?'

'No, no. It's more a musical revue . . . a tribute.' Adelaide began to describe *Broadway Airs*, her dedicated company and the beautiful Sovereign. As she warmed to her subject – the intangible magic of the theatre, the giving, the receiving, the intimate communion between artiste and audience – her passion was utterly contagious, and her listener hung on her every word, captivated.

'Fascinating!' he murmured. 'To be able to sing, to dance, to act . . . to touch so many. I envy you. I confess I'm often tongue-tied in front of even a *small* class.'

'Acting lessons would do wonders for that, you know . . .' Adelaide said absently. She got up and crossed to the window, drawing back the curtain. 'Still snowing,' she sighed. Then, wistfully, she began to croon a little song: '"I'll be with you again, perhaps in the spring . . ."' A sob caught in her throat. 'I wonder how they'll manage without me. I don't suppose I'll ever see them or the theatre again.'

In the flickering glow of the firelight, her damp curls framing her face, Adelaide looked sweetly vulnerable, and Henry thought he had never seen any mouse more beautiful. He set his cup on the table and said resolutely, 'Never say never, my dear! I'll bet my whiskers, you *will* perform tomorrow. By morning I'll have thought of a way to get you home. Trust me.'

CHAPTER 9

Scene Change

THE COMPANY OF *Broadway Airs* had been rehearsing the changes in the programme all evening. Don Q had arranged for meals to be delivered by Nibbles Delicatessen, and the caterers were making every effort to get to the theatre in the snowstorm, which had definitely worsened. Everyone was wondering if there would be enough time to pull the show together by the following night. Even if there was, would any mouse buy a ticket in this weather? Worse still, what if the snow cleared and the demolition of the Sovereign began? Pops reported

that, although hardly any humans were abroad on the street, the wrecking ball was still in place, though almost obliterated by snow.

Enoch suggested that from this point on, the cast and crew remain in the theatre. The company would then be safe from the storm and could put in the necessary overtime. Everyone agreed.

Emil approached Don Q. 'I've had an idea for the finale, Don. See if this works for you. What if we dedicate the entire performance to Adelaide, and at the very end of the show we simply dim the lights in her honour? The rumour mill will undoubtedly have informed everyone of the tragedy, and it would be fitting to show our respect for such a great star . . .'

Don Q thought it a splendid idea. Emil gathered the company and explained the plan. There would be an insert in the programme announcing the moment of silence. Instead of Adelaide's big song, the stage lights would dim, then come up again on the empty staircase. After a suitable pause, the entire company would assemble as planned for 'Sunset Over Broadway'.

His words were received with emotion. The mice children sniffled. Harold blew his nose loudly and wiped his eyes with his handkerchief. Rose and Wendy embraced each other, and Sky patted them both on the back reassuringly. Bernardo and Hysterium clasped hands. Curly looked sad.

Pippin wished that he could somehow alter the dreadful circumstances. He sat on the stage, knees drawn up to his chest, and hung his head, his heart full to bursting. If only he had stayed behind to escort Adelaide indoors after the wrecking-ball incident, or had looked for her in the costume shop

home for opening night, and I'm going to see my first Broadway show! But we have to hurry!'

Adelaide had to smile, for his enthusiasm was infectious. He crooked his arm and cocked his head towards the door. After a moment's hesitation, she linked her arm in his. Braving the icy chill and the swirling snow, they set off.

Less than an hour later, they were perched precariously on the back of a vinyl seat in the cab of a huge snowplough that was making its way slowly into the city. Jostled and thrown off balance, they hung on for dear life as its driver manoeuvred the massive truck forward and backwards, the heavy metal blade of the plough banging and clanging into position, dragging and scraping along the ground as it cleared the snow in its path.

Henry was grinning from ear to ear. 'Isn't this *fun!*' he cried.

Almost deafened by the noise, Adelaide moaned, 'I've already suffered the indignities of one such ride! How much more must I endure?'

'Oh, come now! This is the sort of adventure I've

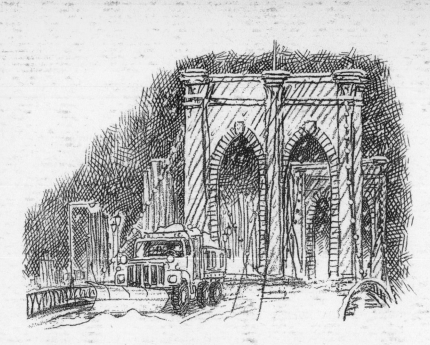

only ever dreamed of! And look!' Henry pointed
with awe at a majestic structure that loomed just
ahead. 'That's got to be the Brooklyn Bridge! I've seen
it in my books! It's magnificent!'

The snowplough rattled on and, as it laboriously
made its way across the great span, the mice thrilled
at the mighty, sweeping curves of steel above them.
The sparkling snow had etched each tower and
cable, and the effect was magical – an ethereal
suspension with no beginning or end, floating in a
misty world of white.

At long last their vehicle rumbled to a stop beside

several other sanitation trucks, and the driver descended from the cab.

In the sudden quiet, Adelaide said, 'Now what?'

'Now . . . we find out where we are,' Henry replied. 'Come on!'

As the mice scrambled down to the slush-covered pavement, Adelaide clapped a paw over her nose. 'Pee-ew! What is that *dreadful* smell?' she exclaimed.

Henry sniffed the air appreciatively. 'Aha! My calculations were correct! This must be the old Fulton Fish Market . . . someone here will be heading uptown.'

'Only a *fool* would be heading *anywhere* in this weather,' Adelaide mumbled miserably as she trotted after him. She wound Henry's scarf tighter around her neck and shivered, for the place was numbingly cold and very damp.

They were beneath a vast overhang of some kind. Forklifts, handcarts and barrows were parked in neat rows, looking like an army of ghostly sentinels. There were boxes and packing crates by the dozen, styrofoam tubs, fibreglass tables, weighing scales, giant ice picks and fish hooks. Yellow plastic aprons hung from big nails along one wall. But there was not a soul to be seen.

'Oh, dear.' Henry stamped his feet and swung his arms in an attempt to stay warm. 'They're obviously closed because of the snow. That's something I never considered. No wonder it's so quiet.' He looked dismayed.

'So much for our luck continuing,' Adelaide declared gloomily.

'*Ni-hao!*' A little voice came from somewhere above their heads. They looked up but could see nothing. The voice came again. 'Hello!' It was a tiny mouse, peering down at them from a tall stack of crates. 'You are looking for something? You are lost?' he asked cheerfully.

'Well, yes, in a manner of speaking,' Henry called. 'Hallo to *you*, good mouse! Could you perhaps help us?'

'Please wait. I will come.' The little mouse disappeared, only to peek moments later around the side of a crate. He was extremely small, with smiling eyes and a jolly demeanour. He wore black trousers and sandals, a mandarin jacket and a little silken cap with a

tassel. 'I am Ping!' he stated. 'Pleased to meet you!'

Henry introduced himself and presented Adelaide. He relayed their predicament and explained how urgent it was that they reach the Sovereign in time for Adelaide's show. Ping's eyes gleamed with interest.

'Oh, yes, indeed! You have a big problem, I can see!' He glanced shyly at Adelaide. 'Very great lady. Very great *honour*.' He bowed. 'A superior mouse must do all he can to assist. I think you must come with me.'

'Where to?' Henry asked, curious.

'I live beneath a human pharmacy, not far from here. I work for my uncle in the mouse apothecary below. I am here to obtain a leech for him, but as you see . . . no one is working today –'

'So?' Adelaide was becoming blue with cold and was more than impatient.

'So, Uncle is very wise. He will most certainly have ideas that can help. My transportation will be leaving momentarily.' Ping pointed to a rickety old rickshaw parked by the wall. It was a contraption much like a three-wheeled bicycle, with a two-wheeled trailer attached to the front that had a collapsible hood over it. 'The human delivery boy is also here for supplies,' Ping continued. 'But I think he will not be lucky either. We can all ride in his trailer. He will not see us.'

'But that's only going a fraction of the distance we have to cover!' Adelaide complained.

Ping smiled sweetly. 'Uncle says . . . "Big things are only achieved by attending to small beginnings."'

'Adelaide, we have to accept whatever opportunity comes our way,' Henry said tactfully as he steered her towards the rickshaw. 'We're lucky to have run into this good mouse. We are most grateful to you, Ping.'

The sound of human footsteps approaching made them all scramble hastily for the trailer. Moments later they were being trundled uptown, their driver pedalling with all his might, puffing and blowing and skidding and skewing on his bike as he pushed through the slippery, thick mush beneath his tyres.

Adelaide groaned. 'How do we even know we're going the right way?'

'Simple!' Henry replied breezily. 'The map indicated we should go north, and that's what we're doing!'

'How do you know *that*?'

'I have a nose for direction. Besides, it's written there – on the lamp post.'

Adelaide looked at him dubiously. 'You're either very smart . . . or completely out of your mind.'

Henry grinned. 'Trust me!'

Ping said, '"A superior mouse is modest in speech but exceeds in actions."'

'I bet your uncle told you that, too?' Adelaide commented drily.

The rickshaw lurched to a halt. As Henry helped her descend, he said, 'Courage, Adelaide. I promised to get you to the theatre on time, and I will. Nothing can stop us now!'

A huge, wet pile of snow slid off the building above their heads and completely doused all three of them.

CHAPTER 10

Act Three

'OHHHH! THE SUN'LL come shining through . . .'
Little June was singing lustily. Dressed as a
young orphan in a simple smock with a wig
of tight red curls upon her head, she stood centre
stage, a friendly cockroach on a lead beside her.

Just as she was heading for the high note, the
loudspeaker system in the auditorium clicked on and
Emil called, 'Hold it, Junie, please! Hold the orchestra!
Is Charlemagne around? I need Charlemagne, if
possible . . .'

The set designer padded on to the stage from the

wings. He was holding a large paintbrush, and his dark clothes were spattered with bright colours. He looked tired and harassed.

'Ah, Charlemagne!' Emil said. 'Is there a reason that only half the backdrop in this number has been painted?'

Charlemagne sniffed. 'I would have thought that was obvious. It isn't finished! It'll be done when I can get to it. I'm doing touch-ups on the stairs right now.'

Emil sounded uptight. 'I think touch-ups can wait, Charlie. Let's get the main things completed. Details are for whatever time we have left.'

'It would *all* be ready if I could be afforded some help.'

'We'll find you the help,' Emil said tersely. 'We *must* proceed, please. We're running dreadfully late.'

Charlemagne trudged offstage, mumbling under his breath. The orchestra began again.

In the wings Curly and Rose were waiting to rehearse the comic duet, which was up next. Sky sauntered over to them. Placing an arm about Rose's shoulder, he said playfully, 'Keep your paws to yourself, Curly, when you're dancing with my girl!'

'If you'll do the same when you're singing with mine,' Curly shot back, and Rose snorted with laughter.

Pippin brought Emil and Enoch mugs of honeyed tea and set them on the technical table. 'Tempers are getting a little frayed, wouldn't you say?' he whispered to Enoch.

Enoch nodded. Frowning with worry, he pressed a button and spoke into his headset, 'Stand by light cue twenty-seven, and twenty-seven, GO!'

Ping's uncle sat on a high stool behind a dusty counter covered with bottles and jars filled with all manner of things: mushrooms, herbs and several grey-looking items that squirmed occasionally. He appeared to be a very old mouse. He had long, white whiskers, and he nodded a great deal. Henry and Adelaide couldn't

tell if he was falling asleep or just being very agreeable. But he had obviously heard everything Ping was saying, for he then launched into a long commentary, the difficulty being that he didn't speak a word of English, so Ping had to translate.

'Uncle says bad weather means dragons are stirring from their sleep. Travel will be v-e-r-r-y difficult. But a journey of a thousand miles must begin with a single step.' Ping's uncle was nodding emphatically. 'He says the subway is normally the quickest way for your journey. But today the line is not running,' Ping went on. 'However' – he raised a paw and smiled – 'Uncle says fortune is on your side. The fireworks store next door is sending a sledge with deliveries for a restaurant in Little Italy. If you hurry, you can catch a ride. This will be one more step towards your destination.'

Henry shook Ping's paw. 'Please thank your uncle very much! We'll go right away. Perhaps our good fortune will continue.'

Ping pressed a tiny vial into Henry's soggy paw. 'For the journey,' he whispered. 'This superior remedy will give strength when needed.'

Adelaide looked up at Ping's uncle, who was still nodding and smiling.

'WE VERY GRATEFUL!' she called loudly, as if he were also deaf. Turning to Ping, she added, 'You have been very kind. I would offer you tickets to my show, but I don't know how you could get there . . . I doubt *we* will.'

Ping bowed. 'A big whirlwind cannot last forever. If

the weather changes, I will come. *Xie-xie!* Thank you! Very great pleasure.'

The sledge at the store next door was piled high with boxes of New Year's Eve sparklers and covered with a tarpaulin. Nearby a well-padded human courier was pulling on gloves and tying the flaps of a hood under his chin.

'I hope we don't bounce too much,' Adelaide whispered wryly as they snuggled down among the packages. 'The friction could set these fireworks off, and we'd be blown out of our boots!'

'Well, we'd maybe reach the theatre a little faster!' Henry joked. 'Goodbye, Ping! So many thanks!'

Their diminutive new friend waved and smiled. '*Zai-jian!* Goodbye!' he called. 'All blessings to you!'

The heavy snow had been piling layer upon layer over the city, and as the courier trudged uptown dragging his combustible cargo, it became impossible to see where the pavement ended and the road began. A salt-spreading truck was trundling to and fro on the empty avenue in a vain attempt to keep the accumulation at bay. The bumpy journey of only ten blocks seemed interminable to Henry and Adelaide, but eventually they sensed the sledge coming to a halt.

Henry peeked out of his hiding place. A big neon sign was blinking above him.

'"Tony's Italian Kitchen",' he read aloud. 'This must be it, Addie. Quick, hop off before we're discovered!' Sinking into the thick carpet of snow, they burrowed their way towards some railings. Avoiding a shovel, which was being wielded by a human in a large pair of wellington boots, they scrambled over the black iron fence, only to tumble unexpectedly down five shallow steps and through the icy bars of a ventilation grille.

They landed with a thud, dazed and drenched, cold and trembling.

'Are you all right?' Henry gasped, reaching for Adelaide.

She nodded. 'So much for good fortune,' she said, wincing.

A robust voice was singing nearby.

'Che gelida ma-nee-naaa . . . !'

Before them was a small door, with a red awning inscribed with the words 'Fausto's Fromaggio'. The door suddenly opened and a portly mouse with a striped apron and a chef's hat upon his head came out and looked at them with surprise.

'*Dio mio!* Customers already? We don't open till lunchtime . . . but since I didn't expect *any* today –' he spread his arms wide '– we will make exceptions! *Avanti*, come in! You look frozen!'

Henry and Adelaide gratefully followed him inside, and their host clapped his hands briskly, flour puffing in little clouds about him as he did so.

'Figaro!' he called. 'We will have *cappuccino!* Where are you? Figaro, Figaro, FEEE-GA-RO!' he sang lustily.

A young mouse popped his head around the door of a tiny kitchen. '*Si, Papa! Pronto!*'

'Tell your brothers and sisters to bring pizza and *cannoli!*' He pulled a napkin from his apron and dusted two chairs set beside a table with a red and white chequered cloth. '*Prego*, make yourselves comfortable! Fausto will take good care of you!'

Adelaide sank into her chair gratefully, unwinding Henry's scarf from around her head.

Fausto took one look at her and clapped his paws to his cheeks.

'Am I dreaming? Is it possible?' he cried. '*Caspita!* It is Adelaide, no? Oh, *bella!* I'm your favourite fan!' He took her paw and kissed it fervently.

Adelaide smiled modestly and patted her hair. 'I'm very flattered . . .'

'I saw you in *Hallo, Mousey!* I will never forget. You were *magnifico!* But what brings you to Fausto's? You are a long way from Broadway!'

Henry and Adelaide explained their desperate situation as a seemingly endless stream of young mice came from the kitchen to ply them with warm and delicious goodies and listen to their amazing tale.

At the conclusion Fausto clutched his forehead, aghast. '*Che disastro!* But you *must* perform tonight! They cannot raise the curtain without you! Can you imagine, *bambinos*? A performance without the great diva! *Momento!* Fausto will think of something!' He paced back and forth, deep in thought. 'Aha!' he cried, brandishing a breadstick. 'I have it! Only one person works outside in weather like this – he is Boris, from the Ukraine! He has a pretzel cart – the best crumbs in town! *Presto*, I will take you! No time to lose!'

Snatching up the last creamy morsel from her plate, Adelaide followed Henry and Fausto through the back of the establishment and down some more steps into an underground sewer.

'It's not the Appia Antica,' Fausto apologized as they skirted some foul-smelling debris. 'But it's the quickest way to Houston Street! Only three blocks to go!' He launched into a rousing operatic song, his voice echoing off the walls of the tunnel, the result being that lurking rats were sent scurrying and Adelaide and Henry were so amused and distracted that they hardly noticed their seamy surroundings or the length of their journey.

Fausto stopped beneath a wrought-iron grating and pointed above him. 'Here – we must climb!' he announced and, panting with the considerable effort, he squeezed his ample frame between the bars. He leaned down to give Adelaide a helping hand, and Henry scrambled after.

They emerged beneath a cart of some kind, supported by two small wheels and two very large ones. A pair of fur-lined snow boots stomped around it, their owner banging and slamming doors as he loaded his merchandise.

'*Buono!* Boris is just leaving. He always goes as far as Fourteenth Street, rain or shine! He has special customers there!' Fausto whispered.

Adelaide gulped. 'But we still have at least thirty blocks to go after *that!*' she said worriedly. 'Oh, we'll *never* make it to the theatre in time . . .'

Henry touched her arm reassuringly. 'Think how

far we've come already, Addie. Ping's uncle said that luck was with us.'

'Ping's uncle wouldn't know a rabbit's foot from a rat's behind.' She turned to their kindly Italian escort. 'Thank you, Fausto. I will never forget your generosity.'

Fausto enfolded her in a crushing hug and kissed her ardently on both cheeks. '*Madonna!* The pleasure is mine. Come to Fausto's Fromaggio any time, and I will sing for you and we will eat.'

'And if, with luck, the snow clears and we *do* make it tonight, I'm sure Addie would love you to see her show,' Henry added pointedly.

Adelaide nodded. 'Of course! There would be seats for you and all the children.'

'And perhaps, a little audition one day?' Fausto winked. He clapped Henry on the shoulder and embraced and kissed him also. 'You are a very lucky man!' he whispered with emotion. 'My heart is full for you both!'

Henry blushed to the tip of his tail. 'Oh – er. Gosh! Well . . . No . . . I'm just a *friend*, actually . . .'

Adelaide pulled at his sleeve. 'Oh, hush up, Henry, and let's get moving. Give me a hand here, will you?'

She launched herself on to the spokes of one of the big wheels and, with Henry's help, carefully climbed on to the warm aluminium plate of the pretzel cart. They wedged themselves at the base of a big umbrella, behind a brown paper bag of salt.

Peering down from their high perch, they smiled at Fausto as he took off his apron and waved it exuberantly.

'*Ciao!*' he cried, then began singing again as Boris shoved his old pretzel cart into motion. 'Goodbye! I wish you all a last GOO-OOODBYE!'

CHAPTER 11

Crescendo

HAROLD STOOD CENTRE stage, dressed as a Russian patriarch, a cap upon his head. He was rehearsing his special solo, singing about what he would do if he had all the cheese in the world.

Sitting at the technical table in the auditorium, Emil leaned into his microphone. 'Hold the orchestra, please — one moment, Maestro!' The music squeaked to a halt. 'Harold, dear . . . is there any way to wear your cap further back on your head? We simply cannot see your eyes. Or can we lose the cap altogether?'

'What?' Harold was flustered. 'Oh . . . oh, right. What shall I do with it, then?'

'Excuse me!' A voice came from the wings, and Mrs Anna, the costume designer, stepped on to the stage. She was small and plump and draped in many layers of clothing, with a tape measure around her neck, pincushions on her wrists and pencils holding up her hair. 'That's a *traditional* costume,' she said tartly, 'and that's the way it's supposed to be worn. There should be a cap on his head . . . but if you're not interested in being *authentic* . . .'

There was a moment's silence, then Emil called again from the darkness of the theatre, 'Harold, darling, *keep* the cap. Just point your face up to the balcony . . . and try not to look at your toes when you're dancing. OK? Continue, please!'

Harold jammed the cap further back upon his head and began singing again. But suddenly he held up both paws, and the orchestra ground to a halt once more. '*Sorry!* But are you getting *any* of this out there?' He pointed to his throat and said dramatically, 'The voice is shot, I'm afraid. If we could maybe find some more of that elderberry wine . . .'

Emil buried his head in his paws.

Enoch took up the microphone. 'We'll get you some lozenges, Harold,' he called. Turning to Pippin, who was sitting beside him, he said urgently, 'Go to Adelaide's dressing room and get him a handful of her throat thingies, will you?'

'You got it!' Pippin rushed backstage and skittered down the corridor to Adelaide's empty room. Bursting through the door, he scanned her dressing table and found the small tin of blackcurrant pastilles. As he picked them up, he caught sight of her red dress hanging alone on the rack, swinging gently in the breeze coming from the hallway. He sighed, wondering where she could be, what she might be doing, or if she was even alive. Though she had always been high maintenance, he suddenly missed Adelaide very much – her larger-than-life personality, her undeniable contribution to the show.

Rushing back to the stage, he delivered the sweets to Harold, who took a large pawful. Clearing his throat, he crammed them all into his mouth. The patient members of the orchestra struck up one more time and, cheeks bulging, he continued his rehearsal.

'Pretzels! Hot pretzels!'

Boris the pretzel man had pulled his cart to a stop in front of a large brick building. A flag with red and white letters emblazoned on it was draped above the door, and uniformed members of a brass band were milling about on the snowy pavement, their breath steamy as they stamped their feet and sorted their musical instruments.

Adelaide peeked around the bag of salt and read the words on the flag. ' "Relief Response Legion." Oh, Henry! I know about these people. I played their missionary lass in our production of *Mice and*

Dolls last year. They do *wonderful* work.'

At the sight of Boris, the musicians surged towards him, cheering his arrival.

'Hooray! Good old Boris!'

'Nothing like warm pretzels to get a Legion band marching on a day like this!'

'We knew you wouldn't let us down!'

'A little snow never bothered Boris!' the pretzel vendor declared as he handed out his wares. 'Here you go! Dese should get you as far as Macy's!'

Amid the laughter and babble of voices, Henry whispered, 'Time to get off, Addie! Watch your whiskers!' Grabbing her paw, he led her over the back of the cart, where they crouched beneath the shadow of one of the wheels.

'I was just beginning to get warm!' Adelaide grumbled. '*Now* what!'

'Give me a moment; I'll come up with something . . .' Henry peered out carefully. 'Look!' he said happily. 'The snow's beginning to ease up a little!' He nearly jumped out of his skin as someone nearby picked up a big bass drum and gave it a mighty *whump!* Tambourines rattled as the marchers got into formation.

'Happy New Year, Boris!'

'See you tomorrow!'

'Macy's, here we come!'

Henry was hit with a sudden inspiration. 'Addie!

See that tuba over there? Quick, make a run for it!'

Before Adelaide could protest, he practically yanked her off her feet, dragging her across the trampled snow and into the gaping mouth of the large musical instrument. Seconds later it was lifted into the air by its owner, and the mice tumbled down inside the ice-cold brass walls to land, trembling, at the bottom of the horn.

'You and your brilliant ideas, Henry!' Adelaide rubbed her bruised backside.

'Adelaide, they said they are going to Macy's. On my map that's Thirty-fourth Street – a whole twenty blocks further north! See, our luck *is* holding!'

'Well, even if by some unlikely miracle I *make* it to the theatre, I'll be so frozen I'll be unable to perform!' Adelaide sneezed. 'Or I'll have caught my death of cold –' She grabbed at Henry for balance as the marcher began to walk at a lively pace, the tuba bouncing and swinging, causing the mice to skid from side to side like soup sloshing in a bowl.

Henry removed one of his sweaters and clumsily pulled it around her shoulders as best he could.

'Trust me . . .' he said for the umpteenth time that day.

'Trust me, trust me, trust me!' Adelaide mumbled miserably. Teeth chattering, she clapped her paws over her ears, for the insistent booming of the bass drum encouraging the walkers was thunderous inside the horn.

Within minutes she was seeing stars and had a pounding headache. Henry was all but deaf in one ear and, by the time the band slowed to a halt twenty blocks later, they were both looking rather green. 'Whew!' Henry gulped, clutching his stomach. 'I guess we're at Macy's! Now, how do we get out of here?'

With a roll of the drums, the enthusiastic musicians struck up a rousing march for the late-afternoon shoppers who had braved the snow for New Year's Eve bargains.

'TA-DA!' blasted the horns, and Henry and Adelaide exploded out of the tuba like confetti.

CHAPTER 12

Show-stopper

THE ORCHESTRA AT the Sovereign was playing stridently, the musicians bravely trying to make sense of the music in front of them. The sound was excruciating, and the entire cast onstage gradually stopped singing, looking confused.

'Hold it! HOLD IT!' Emil was practically tearing his hair out. 'Maestro, *what* is going on? We have two more minutes before we have to break. You've all got the parts, right? You've all got "Sunset Over Broadway"?'

'No, no.' A musician held up a piece of music.

'I've got "Sunrise Over Brooklyn".'

Other musicians nodded. 'Yeah, me too.' 'That's what I have.'

Maestro Maraczek irritably tapped his music stand and said with icy patience, 'Then here's what you do. It's very simple. Put "Sunrise" at the *front* of your books, where it belongs. Now, does anyone have "Sunset" there, by mistake?' A few of the mice nodded again. 'OK. So slip that at the *back* of your books – and the problem should be solved.'

Emil tapped his microphone for attention. 'Listen, everyone, we're completely out of time. We'll have to wing the new ending tonight. You've all been terrific. I'll be backstage to give some notes. Half hour will be called shortly. It's show time, folks! Break a paw!'

As the company and crew disbanded, Curly caught up with Wendy.

'Nervous?' he said.

She nodded.

'Don't be. They're gonna love you,' he said encouragingly, then added shyly, 'as do I.'

* * *

'No, no, NO, Henry!' Adelaide was shouting. 'I cannot go one step further. We've walked only two blocks, and I'm totally exhausted.' Her breath was coming in gasps; her paw was on her chest. 'I don't recognize *anything*. The city is so huge. This is an *endless* nightmare . . .' She sank on to the bottom step of a huge stone staircase.

'Oh, Addie. I'm so sorry. It can't be too much further . . .' Henry looked around. He too was feeling

exhausted, and at this point wasn't even sure if they were still heading in the right direction. He gazed up at the heavens, trying to gauge the time. It was almost dark, and all the lights in the city were beginning to come on.

Suddenly the massive building at the top of the steps behind them blazed into light, revealing columns of supporting pillars, magnificent in their towering splendour. Above a door were the words 'United States Post Office', and on a frieze that spanned the building, a long sentence was carved.

' "Neither snow nor rain nor heat nor gloom of night stays these couriers from the swift completion of their appointed rounds",' Henry read aloud. 'Oh, look, Adelaide! It's a sign! If we could try just a *little* longer . . .'

Adelaide leaned against him wearily. 'Henry, you are very dear. But face it. We're lost. This is the end, I'm afraid, the end of the journey.'

'Don't say that.' Henry took her paw in his. 'I'm hoping this is the beginning of a *new* journey . . . for us.'

Adelaide's eyes were brimming with tears. 'The

curtain will be going up any minute. Oh, I'd love to have made it to the theatre, loved for you to have seen the show. It was very good, you know. It was totally *my* evening.' She sighed, filled with emotion. 'My last song was especially good. I had a beautiful red dress, lots of fringe and sparkle. I descended a grand staircase. I suppose they'll manage without me . . .'

Henry pulled her close.

'You know, Henry,' Adelaide continued, 'in the end, no one is indispensable. There's always someone else who can do what we do just as well, possibly even better.'

'I'm sure no one could replace *you*, Adelaide.'

'Well, yes, perhaps,' she conceded. 'But what's the point, if no one gets to see me?' She pressed her face into his sweater and sobbed. Henry wished he could hug away her sadness.

After a moment she mumbled, 'What's this?' and patted his pocket.

Henry felt with his paw and discovered Ping's vial. 'It's the concoction that Ping gave us! I forgot all about it. Here, my dear. Take it. If nothing else, it might keep you warm.'

Adelaide took a swig from the little bottle.

'Well, the snow has stopped.' She hiccupped. 'At least the revellers in Times Square tonight will be able to enjoy themselves.' She held out the bottle. 'You want some of this? It's not half bad . . .'

Henry shook his head. 'You finish it.'

As Adelaide drained the contents, a large white truck rumbled slowly down the avenue and screeched to a halt at the traffic lights in front of them. Four words emblazoned on the side of it read 'The New York Times'.

Adelaide blinked and sat up. 'Henry! I recognize that truck! It lives in the building right near the Sovereign! HENRY!' She rose to her feet unsteadily. 'I RECOGNIZE THAT TRUCK! It must be going home for the night!'

'Oh, Adelaide! If we could only get aboard! But look – the lights are changing . . . We'll never make it!'

'Am I a professional or aren't I! *Come on*, Henry!' With renewed energy, she bounded ahead of him, leaping across the snow to board the truck just as it started to pull away. Henry scrambled after her, stumbling on the slippery pavement, trying desperately to catch up. The vehicle began to accelerate, changing gears, bouncing and spattering him with muddy slush.

Clinging to the back, Adelaide reached out to him. 'Faster, Henry! *Faster!* Oh, please! I *cannot* do this without you!'

CHAPTER 13

Finale

THE SOVEREIGN WAS was packed to the rafters. In spite of the snow and the freezing cold, the mice who loved Broadway theatre had come out in droves to celebrate New Year's Eve and to see *Broadway Airs: A Tribute to the Great American Mousical.* The excitement in the air was electric. Ushers showed audience members dressed in their holiday finery to their seats. The musicians tuned their instruments in the orchestra pit. There was a buzz of chatter – mice calling greetings and good wishes to each other. Others read their programmes,

in particular the inserted piece of paper that
stated:

> *This evening's performance is dedicated to*
> *the memory of Adelaide.*
> *Prior to the conclusion of our show, please join us*
> *as we honour the greatest leading lady*
> *in mouse theatre with a moment of silence.*

Backstage the dancers stretched and flexed their limbs. Curly and Rose paced out the moves of their duet one last time. Harold did his vocal exercises, one paw on his diaphragm. 'Hip-BAH, hip-BAH!' he intoned, and was delighted to discover that his voice was miraculously restored. Sky slicked back his pomaded hair for the umpteenth time and winked at Rose. Wendy tried to gain control of her nerves by breathing deeply. Hysterium rushed about, adjusting the children's costumes, and Bernardo gave the last flick and touch of spray to the wigs on his wig stands. Pippin dashed from dressing room to dressing room, delivering good-luck bouquets, cards and gifts.

Enoch's voice came over the loudspeaker backstage. 'Places, please, for the top of act one! Good show, everyone!'

Five minutes later, the house lights dimmed. The magnificent chandelier above the auditorium faded to a soft glow. Maestro Maraczek raised his baton for attention and, with a flourish, brought it down to begin the rousing overture.

Assembled behind the great red stage curtain, the

company touched paws for luck, whispering encouragements, clearing throats.

Harold murmured, '" The die is cast . . ."'

At the back of the audience, Emil and Don Q glanced nervously at each other, knowing that there was nothing more they could do to help – it was up to their cast and crew to deliver a performance worthy of the occasion: the closing night of a great theatre.

And what a performance it was!

Rose and Curly's comic dance routine drew roars of laughter. Sky and Wendy's love duet was a smash. The mice children performed their number flawlessly, eliciting sentimental 'Ohhhs' and 'Aaahs' from the adoring audience. Little June sang with gusto; everyone loved Curly's brilliant soft-shoe. Harold's solo was a master class in stagecraft – each nuance of his character played to perfection. Looking enchanting in her flower-girl costume, Wendy sang Adelaide's song about a warm and cosy place, and the audience gave her touching rendition the ovation it deserved.

During the interval Harold padded into Adelaide's dressing room to grab another handful of lozenges.

Gazing down at her table, he lovingly brushed a paw across her make-up items and silver-handled hairbrushes. If only she could have been with them this evening!

Glancing in the mirror, he whispered gently, 'We're a hit, Addie. "A very palpable hit."'

With a sigh, he reached into the pastille tin. Just as his paw closed around the throat-soothing goodies, the dressing-room door flew open with a crash. He spun around guiltily. Then, wide-eyed and boggled, he gasped and, legs suddenly weak, he felt himself falling, falling . . . and he sank to the floor in a faint.

Act two continued to wow the audience. Maestro Maraczek pulled miracles of sound from his orchestra. Enoch, Fritz and Pippin worked furiously backstage – giving cues; pulling ropes; helping with scenery, props and quick changes. But in spite of the effort and the individual accomplishments, everyone in the company could feel that the show was missing one key element – the star turn that would bring down the house and elevate the evening into the realm of the sublime.

Inevitably *Broadway Airs* neared its finale, and the difficult and painful tribute to Adelaide was at hand. The stage curtains slowly came together, and the lights dimmed. The orchestra sustained a trembling chord. Heads bowed, the audience appeared to hold its breath as one, silently remembering the glowing star who had given so much pleasure to so many through the years.

Then, with a ripple of velvet, the curtains swung open again and – miracle of miracles – she was there!

At the top of the grand golden staircase, Adelaide stood bathed in the spotlight, resplendent and radiant in her sparkling red dress. A collective intake of breath rolled through the auditorium. Maestro Maraczek froze, astonished. Then, recovering, he quickly alerted the orchestra to the different cue and, as her signature music blasted out, Adelaide slowly and gracefully began to descend and sing to her 'boys'.

'Hallo-o-o, fellas! Addie's back in town!'

The audience went wild – stomping, yelling, screaming. The company, rushing to the wings to witness the moment, cheered and wept openly. In the first row of the balcony, Ping smiled and nodded, and Fausto was standing up, blowing endless kisses to

the stage and yelling, *'Brava! Brava!'* Mrs Fausto had to retrieve their children, who were almost tumbling over the railing in their excitement.

Sweet Henry, still spattered with mud, blinked furiously and wiped his glasses. Slack-jawed with admiration and bursting with pride, he watched his beloved give the performance of her life. As Adelaide raised her arms for the final note of the song, the ovation was so thunderous that the roof practically lifted off the building. It was thrilling – and deeply moving. This night would live forever in Broadway legend.

CHAPTER 14

Bows

THE CRIES OF 'ENCORE!', the shouts and the roars gave way to a babble of chatter and a crush of mice backstage after the show. Adelaide was being hugged and kissed by everyone.

Fully resuscitated, Harold was being fussed over and fanned by two pretty mice from the chorus. 'I thought she was a ghost!' he was saying. 'She was barely recognizable, spattered in mud, torn and tattered, shivering with cold! I was convinced she wasn't real, and then, "O, wonderful, wonderful, and most wonderful, wonderful!" — she spoke!

That beautiful, unforgettable voice said –'

'"Harold, you twit, get your paws off my pastilles!"' Adelaide finished the sentence for him.

Amid the laughter that followed, he got up and joyously swung her off her feet with a giant hug. She spotted Henry lurking shyly on the periphery of the crowded dressing room.

'Everyone! Quiet a moment. *That* is the one you should be applauding. That darling mouse is responsible for my being here . . . for giving me back my life.' Adelaide described everything that had happened – the disastrous moment of her capture, the meeting with Henry and their incredible journey back into Manhattan – and the mice listened to her tale with awe. By the time she had finished, Henry was

swept up in a wave of gratitude. Lifting him shoulder high, the company cheered, patted and thumped him – and sang a rousing version of 'For He's a Jolly Good Rodent'. Nodding, smiling, blushing and adjusting his spectacles, which were askew on his nose, Henry good-naturedly accepted the warmth and affection that welcomed him into the Broadway mouse family.

'OK, everyone, listen up!' Emil called. 'Let us all go out to Times Square and watch the silver ball come down at midnight. This may have been the last performance in our beloved Sovereign, but after tonight *nothing* can break our company apart. We will go on somehow and, one day, we will look back on this as a new beginning. Let's *celebrate!*'

Pippin was among the last to leave the theatre. He stood on the empty stage and, for a moment, fancied he could still hear the echo of the evening's applause and cheers. What an extraordinary night it had been! It was thrilling that their final performance had been such a stunning success, but at the same time he felt deeply sad. Realizing that it was the last time he would see the theatre, he blew a kiss in the direction of the auditorium, switched on the ghost light, and turned away, blinking tearfully.

' "Our revels now are ended . . ." ' Harold's voice came from the wings. The kindly actor came onstage and put an arm around Pippin's shoulders. 'Come, lad. Put away your sorrow. We have a new year ahead of us, and who knows what it may bring. Let us go up and join the others. There is nothing more we can do here.'

They walked slowly and silently down the corridor to the stage door, where Pops was putting on his jacket. As the three mice exited their little theatre and climbed the stairs to the big theatre above, the human stage door suddenly swung open, scattering ice and debris into the hallway. Startled, Pippin, Harold and Pops quickly scuttled beneath the radiator. They heard footsteps walking towards them, and – horrifyingly – they stopped right where the mice were hiding.

'Dad! I *know* the ball has to be here somewhere. It'll only take a minute to look for it. We'll still make it outside by midnight . . .'

'Go ahead, son. It's your last chance, I guess. Demolition starts tomorrow.'

'I know. I wish it didn't have to.'

Pippin recognized the voices. Turning to Harold and Pops, he held up a paw for silence, then nearly squeaked aloud – for, right next to them, wedged at the back of the radiator, was the boy's elusive baseball.

All at once an idea exploded in his head.

Quickly whispering instructions to Harold and Pops and begging them to do as he asked, Pippin pushed down his fear and took a deep, steadying breath. Then, carefully, he nudged the ball out into the hallway and sent it rolling towards the steps of the basement. His heart pounding, he scampered after it, Pops and Harold following in hot pursuit. They disappeared into the darkness of the stairwell.

Startled, the adult voice said, 'Ugh! Dratted mice!'

'Hey, Dad! My ball!' The boy ran towards it with delight, but before he could retrieve it, Harold inched forward to nose it gently over the edge of the first

step. It bounced — *plop, plop, plop* — down to the landing below. The boy chuckled and went after it again, cautiously feeling his way down the stairs.

'Son? Where are you going?'

'I'll be right back, Dad!'

He reached the first landing, his feet within centimetres of Pops's whiskers. It was the elder mouse's turn to nudge the baseball on its way once more. It rolled again, bouncing another steep flight to lodge in a corner at the bottom.

The boy's feet slipped on the concrete steps as he scrambled after it.

'Are you OK, son?'

'I'm fine!'

Pippin was waiting for him. A mere fraction of a second before the boy's hand reached to pick it up, the little mouse darted out, jiggled the ball into position, and gave it one last shove.

He held his breath as he watched it teeter for the longest moment. Then, seemingly in slow motion, it rolled over to thud from step to step. Gaining speed, it finally disappeared altogether into the darkness of the vaulted basement.

The boy looked down the last flight and hesitated.

Pippin crossed his paws, closed his eyes and wished a fervent wish . . . and the boy continued on.

There was silence.

'Son? Son! Are you there?'

'DAD!'

'What is it? Where are you? Are you hurt?'

'No! No, I'm OK. But . . . can you come down here a moment? There's something I *really* think you should see . . .'

CHAPTER 15

Celebration

TIMES SQUARE WAS a tumult of New Year's Eve sound and commotion. A band was playing somewhere, and there was a cacophony of rattles, buzzers and whistles and the harsh blare of trumpets and tin mouth cones.

A long line of people danced a conga, their feet swinging from side to side.

'Pah-dom, pom, pom, ta-pom, DAH! Pah-dom, pom, pom, ta-pom, DAH!'

Dancing among and around their feet, the Broadway mice emulated the human steps, performing their

own conga line and, strangely, no one seemed to notice or mind. Mice children were squeaking and giggling with delight as Bernardo did his own wacky interpretation of the dance.

'Emil! Enoch!' Pippin burst on to the scene, with Harold and Pops in breathless pursuit. 'Fritz! Curly! ANYONE!' Pippin was yelling at the top of his lungs, desperately scanning the crowd. It was hard to make himself heard, and he pushed his way through the crush of human feet and mice.

'Pippin!' Enoch was shoving mice aside in an attempt to reach him. 'What is it, Pippin? What's the matter?'

'Oh, ENOCH! You'll *never* guess what's happened! I have the most amazing news!'

'News? What sort of news?'

'Yes, what? What?' The mice children jostled each other and crowded around Pippin. The young apprentice gasped for breath, then yelled again.

'We don't have to worry any more! Our theatre isn't going to be torn down! I saved it!'

'You WHAT?' Enoch could barely hear him.

'I SAVED OUR THEATRE!'

'You didn't!'

'I did. I DID!'

'NO!'

'YES!'

Enoch was speechless.

'He certainly did!' Harold's stentorian voice cut through the noise of the festivities. 'Our Pippin, here, has brought about a miracle.'

Enoch beckoned furiously to Emil and Don Q. 'Quickly, *quickly*, come here!' he shouted, and waved to Rose, Curly, Wendy, Sky and everyone else to do the same.

Harold and Pops took it in turns to relate the wondrous happening. Thanks to Pippin's brilliant idea to use the baseball as a lure, the new owner of the theatre and his son had discovered the little model of the Sovereign in the basement. They were surprised and amazed at its beauty, seeing for the first time what the lovely theatre had once looked like.

'The father had heard of the original model but thought it had been destroyed, lost forever —' Harold explained.

'They spoke of cancelling the demolition tomorrow and of restoring and preserving the *whole place*!' Pippin broke in. 'The boy *begged* his dad to save it! He was terrific! He said it could become a New York City landmark — a treasure!'

'Oh, PIPPIN!' Wendy hugged him delightedly. 'But weren't you scared? What if something had happened to you?'

'But it didn't!' Pippin beamed. 'I figured it couldn't do

any harm to let them find our theatre. It was going to be destroyed . . . and there was just *maybe* a chance that they would realize how special it is . . . and they DID!'

'They did! *They did!*' The mouse children danced about, hugging him, hugging one another. Charlemagne and Mrs Anna were hugging. All the pretty chorus mice were hugging Harold. Wendy and Curly were kissing. Rose and Sky were kissing. Enoch and his wife were kissing. Bernardo was kissing everyone, including Hysterium. And in the middle of it all, Henry was kissing Adelaide.

So, our story ends where it really all began . . . beneath a starry sky, amid the beautiful, blazing lights of Times Square – the Great White Way, as it is sometimes fondly called.

Don Q took Emil aside, and they talked earnestly together.

'You know, Emil, it occurs to me that until our beloved Sovereign has been renovated, we're going to need a temporary venue for our productions.'

'You must have read my mind,' Emil concurred.

'What would you say if we relocated to the park for a while? I've been thinking of doing something there along the lines of free public theatre for all mice.'

Emil's eyes widened. 'Why, that's brilliant! We'd have no trouble establishing a new stage . . . there are so many possible venues.'

'I know.' Don Q nodded, satisfied. He looked across at Pippin, who was playing with Enoch's children, swinging them at arm's length, around and around. 'I'll be needing an assistant. What's your opinion of the lad there — young Pippin? He seems a smart fellow.'

'Oh, indeed he is! It is *amazing* what he pulled off tonight . . . that a mouse, so small, could do something so monumental, for so many.'

'My thoughts exactly.'

Enoch was waving at them, yelling, 'LOOK!' He pointed upward.

The shining silver ball on top of the tall building was beginning its slow, sparkling descent. Over the noise of fireworks popping, the deliriously happy crowd began the ever-familiar countdown:

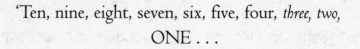

'Ten, nine, eight, seven, six, five, four, *three, two,*
ONE . . .

HAPPY NEW YEAR!'

Glossary of Theatrical Terms

air – song; melody.

aisle – a passageway between the sections of seats in a theatre.

applause – approval or praise for a performance, shown by clapping hands.

apprentice – a novice student, working as an assistant in order to gain experience.

apron – the front part of the stage, which extends beyond the 'picture frame' or proscenium arch; the part of the stage nearest the audience.

audition – an acting and/or singing and/or dancing test, to determine the most suitable performer for a part in a show.

auditorium – the area in a theatre where the audience sits; sometimes called the house.

backdrop – a flat curtain hung at the back of the stage, often painted to represent a scene.

backstage – the area beyond the stage, invisible to the audience. It includes the wings, dressing rooms and wardrobe.

baritone – a male singer with a medium-low voice.

baton – the slender stick used by a musical director when conducting an orchestra.

benefit – a performance that raises money for a charitable cause.

'Break a paw!' (**'Break a leg!'**) – 'Good luck!' Theatre folk are famously superstitious. It is considered unlucky to say 'Good luck!' to an actor before a performance, so the phrase 'Break a leg!' is commonly used instead. The expression has been around since the 1920s, but its origins are unknown.

Broadway – a long diagonal avenue that runs through New York City, at the centre of which many of the great theatres are clustered. The term is also used to refer to the New York theatre industry itself.

cast – the members of the acting company in a show.

character – an individual role in a play or story.

character actor – an actor who specializes in quirky or eccentric roles.

choreographer – the creator of the dance movements in a show.

company – the entire group involved with a production; the cast, crew and creative team combined.

costume shop – the room backstage where the costumes are stored, maintained and sometimes built; also called wardrobe department.

costumes – the clothes worn during a play or performance.

creative team – the artistic leadership of a production – the director, author, choreographer, musical director and all the designers – who make the creative decisions about a show.

crescendo – in music, a gradual increase in loudness or intensity.

crew – the technical team who work backstage to make the show happen: the stage manager, assistant stage managers, dressers, stagehands, sound and lighting technicians, and other members of the running crew. *See* running crew.

cue – a bit of dialogue, action or music, or a signal from the stage manager that prompts the next thing to happen onstage.

curtain call – the end of a show, when the actors come out to take their bows.

director – the one responsible for the overall vision of the production: the way the story is told, what it looks like, where and when the actors move and how they say their lines.

diva – an exceptional leading lady singer.

dress rehearsal – the final rehearsal of a play or musical, where everything is put together and performed as if it were a public performance.

dressing room – a room backstage where actors get dressed, style their hair and put on make-up.

drop – a piece of canvas or fabric that is used either as a painted scene behind the actors, or to hide scenery being changed behind it.

duet – a song for two characters to sing together.

'Encore!' – from the French word meaning 'again'. This is what audience members shout during the applause, when they are particularly pleased and want more.

ensemble – a group of musicians, dancers or actors who perform together with roughly equal contributions from all members; the additional company members who support the stars and principals. Also sometimes called 'the chorus'.

entr'acte – a piece of music performed between acts of a play, musical or opera.

facade – the front, or 'face', of a building.

fanfare – a flourish of trumpets to signal an entrance or a beginning.

finale – the final number of a show or musical.

footlights – a row of lights along the front of the stage.

ghost light – a caged light bulb on a stand, left burning onstage overnight to ensure safety in a dark theatre.

Green Room – a room where the actors meet, relax, have refreshments or wait before or during the performance. No one knows for sure the origin of the term, but one of many theories is that 'greengage' ('green' for short) is cockney-rhyming slang for 'stage', so a room by the stage was a 'green' room.

half hour – the time exactly half an hour before the curtain rises, when all actors must have reported to the theatre to begin dressing and getting ready for the performance. The stage manager calls 'half hour' as the first of a series of warnings to the company as curtain time approaches. Subsequent calls given are 'fifteen minutes', 'five minutes', and 'places' just prior to 'curtain up'.

headdress – a covering or decoration for the head, often quite elaborate.

headset – a headphone with a small microphone attached, worn by the backstage crew to communicate quietly with each other during the show.

house – a theatre term for either the audience (as in 'How big is the house tonight?') or the auditorium (as in 'The house is now open', meaning audience members are coming in).

house lights – the lights in the auditorium of a theatre that fade when the performance starts.

ingénue – a young actress, usually pretty and innocent-looking; the young romantic leading lady.

interval – the fifteen- to twenty-minute pause or break between acts in a play or musical.

lead/leading lady/leading man – the actor or actress who plays the principal role in a production.

lens – the piece of curved glass that protects the bulb in a theatre light and helps soften or focus the light.

lobby – the public waiting area in a theatre, where the audience gathers before going in to see the show.

maestro – a master of any art, especially music.

number – a song and/or dance routine in a musical performance.

opening – the first official public performance of a show.

orchestra – all the musicians who play for a show.

orchestra pit – the space in front of and/or below the stage, where the orchestra performs.

orchestra stalls – the seating area closest to the stage.

ovation – enthusiastic, sustained applause. A standing ovation is when the audience also rises to its feet.

overtime – any time beyond the regular eight-hour rehearsal day, when the company must be paid extra for working longer than usual.

overture – a musical introduction; an instrumental medley of songs (which will be heard later in the show) played as the lights fade and before the curtain rises.

'Places'/'Places, please' – the stage manager's call for actors to get into position for the start of the show.

producer – the one who raises the money, hires the company, pays their salaries and coordinates all the activities in connection with putting on a show.

production – a show, play or work produced for an audience.

programme – a printed booklet of information about the show and its company members. Also called a playbill or showbill.

programme insert – a page inserted into the programme announcing unexpected changes or additions to the show.

prompt corner – the area from which the stage manager controls ('prompts') the performance.

props – short for 'properties'; any of the small movable objects used as part of the stage business, such as teacups, books, pillows or umbrellas.

proscenium/proscenium arch – the arch framing the stage within which the audience observes the performance.

quick change – a very fast costume change that a performer makes during a performance. Quick changes usually take place on the side of the stage in a makeshift booth to save going back to a dressing room.

rehearsal – a practice for a play or show, or any part of it.

revue – a type of musical performance usually consisting of songs, dances and comic sketches, but without a central story.

role – the character an actor plays in a performance.

routine – a well-rehearsed and frequently performed theatrical number.

running crew – the technical staff who run the show backstage during the performance, assisting with scene and costume changes, props, actors' cues and so on.

scenery – the built and/or painted elements used onstage to help the audience understand where a show or scene is taking place.

script – the written dialogue, action and stage directions of a play or musical.

seamstress – a woman who sews costumes.

set – the scenery and props arranged together onstage to suggest where the show or scene is taking place. *See* props, scenery.

show-stopper – something in a show (often a song or dance) so exciting that applause from the audience interrupts the performance.

signature music – a musical phrase or song that has come to be associated with a certain performer or the character he or she plays.

soubrette – a pretty, fun-loving female character who plays a supporting role.

soft-shoe – a smooth kind of tap dance performed with soft leather shoes.

solo – a performance done by one individual.

stage door – the backstage entrance to the theatre, used by the actors and other members of the company.

stage manager – the director's second-in-command; in charge of everything backstage during rehearsal and performances.

stagecraft – the art of crafting, writing or performing for the stage.

stagehand – someone who works backstage, moving scenery and props, operating the curtains, lights and so on during a performance.

stalls – the ground-floor seats in a theatre.

supporting – an actor or role secondary to the lead or principal.

technical table/tech table – a temporary table set up in the auditorium of the theatre, where the director, stage manager and designers sit and work during technical rehearsals. Once the show is up and running, the tech table is removed.

technician – someone who works on the technical part of the show, such as running the computerized lighting board or sound equipment, or operating the spotlight.

tiers – a series of seats, arranged one above the other.

touch-ups – last-minute improvements or finishing touches made to the scenery, costumes, make-up and so on.

tribute – a performance given to honour someone.

usher – someone who shows audience members to their seats in a theatre.

venue – a place where performances are held; another word for theatre or performance hall.

wardrobe department – the place where theatrical costumes are stored, maintained and sometimes built. Also called costume shop.

warm up – to practise or exercise the body or voice in preparation for a performance.

wings – the areas to either side of a stage, out of sight of the audience, where actors wait to make an entrance, or where scenery is stored.